Pet Friends Forever

The Great Kitten Challenge

by Diana G. Gallagher

illustrated by Adriana Isabel Juárez Puglisi

Raintree

Raintree is an imprint of Capstone Global Library Limited,
a company incorporated in England and Wales having its registered office at 7 Pilgrim
Street, London, EC4V 6LB - Registered company number: 6695582

www.raintreepublishers.co.uk
myorders@raintreepublishers.co.uk

Edited by Helen Cox Cannons
Designed by Kristi Carlson and Philippa Jenkins
Original illustrations © Capstone Global Library Ltd 2014
Image Credits: Shutterstock/Kudryashka (pattern)

Originated by Capstone Global Library Ltd
Production by Helen McCreath
Printed and bound in China

ISBN 978 1 406 27966 5
18 17 16 15 14
10 9 8 7 6 5 4 3 2 1

British Library Cataloguing in Publication Data
A full catalogue record for this book is available from the British Library.

All the internet addresses (URLs) given in this book were valid at the time of going to
press. However, due to the dynamic nature of the internet, some addresses may have
changed, or sites may have changed or ceased to exist since publication. While the
author and publisher regret any inconvenience this may cause readers, no responsibility
for any such changes can be accepted by either the author or the publisher.

TABLE OF CONTENTS

1

Rex runs away

Usually when Kyle Blake played fetch with Rex, his yellow Lab, the dog brought the ball straight back so Kyle could throw it again.

But today Rex had other plans. Instead of returning the ball, the yellow Lab stopped, ball still in his mouth, a metre away from where Kyle sat. He stared at Kyle and wagged his tail, but he didn't drop the ball. When Kyle reached out to take it, Rex took off running.

"Rex, come back here!" Kyle called, laughing.

Rex ignored him and ran in circles around the garden. He flipped his head, tossed the ball and caught it when it bounced. He eventually stopped in front of Kyle again, but took off the instant Kyle moved.

Kyle sighed. Rex wasn't in the mood to listen today.

Just then, Kyle's best friend, Mia Perez, walked up. She lived next door, and since it was Saturday, they'd made plans to hang out together. "What's the matter?" she asked.

"Rex isn't following the rules for playing fetch," Kyle said.

As if he was determined to prove Kyle right, Rex raced in big circles around both children. Kyle tried to catch him and ended up belly flopping in the dirt.

Mia laughed. "He's having too much fun to play by the rules," she said.

"Well, I like playing ball too much to let him get away with it," Kyle said. He stood up and brushed off his T-shirt and jeans, which were now covered in dirt.

"What are you going to do?" Mia asked, still giggling.

"Remind Rex that he's the dog, and I'm the person," Kyle said firmly. "That means I'm the boss."

But before Kyle could do anything, Rex trotted over to where they stood and dropped the ball at Mia's feet.

Mia giggled and held onto the dog's collar. "I've got him," she said.

"Let's take him for a W-A-L-K," Kyle suggested, opening the back door. "I'll get the L-E-A-S-H." He headed inside. Rex pulled away from Mia and barked at the door.

When Kyle came back outside, he hid the leash behind his back. The dog whined and turned in excited circles.

Mia laughed. "I don't think you're fooling him," she said. "Rex is too smart. He knows what we're doing."

"Maybe he's learnt how to spell!" Kyle said.

"I guess that means we need new code words," Mia said.

Kyle was glad Rex was so smart, but sometimes it got the dog into trouble.

"Rex, sit!" Kyle commanded again.

Thankfully, this time Rex listened. As soon as Kyle attached the leash to the dog's collar, Rex lunged towards the gate. He pulled Kyle all the way across the garden to the pavement.

"Heel!" Kyle said.

Rex pulled. Kyle tugged on his collar and repeated the command until Rex finally slowed down and walked by Kyle's side.

Mia sighed. "I wish cats were as easy to train as dogs," she said. Her cat, Misty, was always getting into trouble.

"Is Misty being bad?" Kyle asked. "More than usual, I mean."

"Yes!" Mia exclaimed, shaking her head. "She keeps playing with shampoo bottles in the bath."

"What's wrong with that?" Kyle asked. "Plastic bottles don't break."

"But the tops come off," Mia said. "Or Misty claws holes in them. Then she leaves sticky paw prints all over the place. And it takes forever to get a whole bottle of shampoo suds out of a bath."

Kyle and Mia came to a stop at the corner. On the opposite side of the street, the empty buildings and woods looked dark and gloomy, even during the day.

"He knows 'sit' and 'heel'," Kyle said. "Let's see if he remembers how to stay."

Kyle held a hand out in front of Rex's nose. "Rex, sit," he said.

Rex sat and looked up at Kyle, wagging his tail back and forth. Kyle set Rex's long, retractable leash down, and Mia put her foot on it, just in case.

"Stay," Kyle instructed. Then he turned and walked down the pavement. Rex stayed right where he was.

Kyle stopped a metre away and turned back to face Mia and Rex. "Come!" he said.

Mia lifted her foot off the leash, and Rex trotted right over and stopped in front of him.

"Good boy!" Kyle said. He leaned over to pick up Rex's leash. Suddenly, Rex took off running towards the empty buildings. His retractable leash stretched to its limit, pulling Kyle after him.

"Rex, stop!" Kyle shouted, chasing after his dog. "Heel!"

Mia raced after them and caught up to Rex and Kyle just as the dog came to a stop in front of an old shed partially hidden in the trees. Rex stood in front of the door barking at something inside.

"What's in there?" Mia whispered.

"I don't know," Kyle muttered. "But if Rex is sounding the alarm, it can't be good."

2

Alone in the dark

"Quiet, Rex!" Kyle said, trying to keep his voice down. He definitely didn't want whatever Rex was barking at in the shed to hear him. Especially since they didn't know what it was yet. He grabbed Rex's collar and tried to pull the dog away from the door, but Rex wouldn't budge.

"Maybe there's a snake inside," Mia suggested. She shuddered at the thought. She didn't mind seeing pet snakes, but she definitely didn't want to run into one in the wild. Especially in this dark, abandoned shed. "Or a raccoon."

"Or a skunk," Kyle said, making a face. It wouldn't be the first time Rex had found a skunk.

A few months ago, Rex had found one sniffing around the back garden and decided to investigate. He was always up for making friends with new animals. But the skunk hadn't been feeling quite as friendly. He'd sprayed Rex. It had taken Kyle hours to scrub the smell off in the bath.

Rex suddenly stopped barking and sniffed at the door. Kyle put his finger to his lips. Mia nodded in agreement, and they both listened, but the only sound they heard was Rex's loud sniffing.

"It might not be something scary," Mia said. "Maybe it's just something quiet."

"Like what?" Kyle asked. He was a little nervous, too, but he didn't want Mia to know.

Mia shrugged. "Maybe it's a ghost?" she suggested.

"I don't think dogs can smell ghosts," Kyle said.

Rex whined again and pawed at the door to the shed.

"Maybe not, but he definitely smells something," Mia said.

Kyle moved a little closer to the shed. "Did you hear that?" he asked, putting his ear to the door.

"What?" Mia asked as she moved up next to him.

"It sounded like something was crying," Kyle said. He grabbed the door handle and pulled it towards him just a little. The rusty hinge squeaked loudly in protest as the door opened a crack.

Rex whined.

"What is it?" Mia asked, peering over Kyle's shoulder.

"I don't know," Kyle said. "It's too dark in there to see anything. There's only one way to find out."

Kyle pulled the door the rest of the way open and looked inside. As sunlight flooded the shed, he gasped as he caught sight of what Rex had already smelled.

3

A surprising discovery

"It's kittens," Kyle said. "Come here and look!"

Mia squeezed into the doorway next to him to get a better look. "Oh, they're so cute!" she said.

In the corner of the cluttered, dirty shed, three little balls of fluff – two orange and one grey – were sleeping on a dirty towel.

"They're so tiny!" Kyle exclaimed. "I hope they're not sick."

One of the orange kittens opened its eyes and meowed quietly. It seemed almost too weak to move much.

"I wonder where their mother is," Mia said, looking around.

"I don't know," Kyle said, "but I think we should probably go get my mum." Kyle's mother was a vet with her own clinic. She'd know what was wrong with the kittens and what they should do.

"You stay here with Rex and the kittens," Mia said. "I'll go and get your mum and be right back."

After Mia left, Rex stretched out so his nose almost touched the kittens. Kyle kept an eye out in case the mother cat decided to return. While he waited, he gently petted the three kittens.

Soon, Mia returned with Kyle's mum. They were carrying a box, towels, dishes, cat food and water.

"Let's see what we have here," Kyle's mum said. She carefully picked up the kittens and placed them on a clean towel inside the box.

"Why would their mother just leave them here?" Mia asked.

"She might be out hunting," Dr Blake said. "Or something could have happened to her that kept her from coming back."

Dr Blake put the dishes on the floor of the shed. She filled one with cat food and the other with water. "We'll leave food in case the mother comes back," she said. "That way, she'll keep coming back even though the kittens are gone."

"Are we taking them home with us?" Kyle asked.

"We're taking them to the clinic so I can give them a check-up," his mum said. "That way we can at least feed them in case their mother doesn't come back. Good thing you two found them when you did!"

Kyle and Mia gave each other a thumbs-up. Then Kyle patted Rex's head. "You're a hero, Rex," he said.

Rex wagged his tail, but he didn't take his eyes off the kittens.

4

Okay for now

Dr Blake carried the box with the kittens into the clinic and down a short hallway to the exam rooms. "I asked Angie to get one of the rooms ready before I left, just in case," she explained.

They pushed open the door to the first exam room. Angie Gorman, the vet tech, was waiting there to help.

Mia followed them into the room, but Kyle paused in the doorway.

"Rex, you can't come in," he said. He grabbed Rex's collar and started to lead him down the hall, but the dog let out a loud whine.

"It's okay, Rex can come in," Dr Blake said. "But he has to be quiet."

Kyle let go of Rex's collar, and the dog immediately trotted into the exam room. He sat down next to the exam table and gazed up at the box of kittens sitting on top of it, watching them closely.

"Are the kittens going to be okay?" Mia asked, looking worried.

"I'll know more after I examine them," Dr Blake said, "but I think so. They look pretty healthy."

"I bet Rex found them just in time," Kyle said. He reached down to scratch Rex behind his ears. Rex rolled his head back and let his tongue hang out in appreciation.

"Do you know how old they are?" Mia asked.

Dr Blake picked up the largest kitten and looked at its teeth. The kitten squirmed in her hands. "This little guy is about seven weeks old," she said.

"Is that old enough to eat normal cat food?" Kyle asked.

"Yes, they can drink water and eat kitten food," Dr Blake replied. She was quiet for a moment as she listened to the kitten's heart and checked its ears.

When she was done, Dr Blake picked up the second yellow tabby and examined it. "I think we should plan to give them kitten formula for a few days, though. That will help them get stronger faster," she explained.

"We'll need to bottle feed them at first since they're so little," Angie added, holding up a tiny baby bottle.

Dr Blake finished checking the second kitten and picked up the third one. The grey-and-white kitten was only half the size of its two siblings.

"Mia and I can feed them," Kyle offered. "We don't mind, do we, Mia?"

"Not at all," Mia agreed. "I'd love to help take care of them. I already have plenty of experience from taking care of Misty when she was a baby."

"I don't know," Angie said. "They'll need formula every three hours."

"No problem," Kyle said. "The kittens can stay in my room, and–"

"The kittens will stay here in the clinic, where I can check on them," his mum interrupted.

"But Mia and I want to take care of them," Kyle protested.

"You and Mia can clean the cage and feed them before and after school," his mum replied. "Angie and I will take care of them at night."

"I'll take a night shift, too," Lillian, Dr Blake's receptionist, offered from the doorway. "How are they?"

"They need medicine for ear mites and worms," Dr Blake said. "Time and food should take care of the rest. And then they'll need homes."

"I wish I could have one," Mia said. "But Misty doesn't like other cats."

"Misty doesn't like anything!" Kyle exclaimed. "She hates Rex, and she hisses at me."

"She likes me!" Mia said. "That's all that matters."

"I'd love to take one, but we have three dogs," Angie said. "And they love to chase cats."

"We'll have to put up a sign in the office," Dr Blake said. "Maybe one of our other patients will be interested. It looks like we've got two boys and one grey-and-white girl. They're cute, so it shouldn't be too hard to find someone who's interested in taking them home."

"Are you two ready to feed them?" Angie asked.

"Yes!" Kyle and Mia answered.

Kyle didn't ask if he could have a kitten.
He was happy with Rex. Besides, his mum was
right. The kittens were so cute that finding
good homes would be easy.

Gone!

The next morning, Kyle's alarm went off bright and early. He rolled over and looked at the clock. For a minute, Kyle was confused. It was only six a.m. Why was his alarm going off so early?

Suddenly, he remembered – it was time to feed the kittens!

Kyle hit the off button and jumped out of bed. He quickly got dressed and ran downstairs to the kitchen. He had to feed Rex before he went anywhere else.

His mum was already in the kitchen fixing a cup of coffee when he came in.

"I'll be ready to head to the clinic in a second," Kyle said.

"Okay," his mum said with a smile. "I'm glad to see you're being so responsible about taking care of the kittens."

"Rex found them, so that makes them my responsibility," Kyle said as he poured dog food into Rex's bowl. Rex finished it off almost before Kyle finished pouring it. "Ready when you are."

Kyle's mum always went to the clinic early. She had to check on the animals that had stayed overnight. Some of them were recovering from operations. Luckily, her clinic was right next to their house, so they didn't have far to walk.

Mia was waiting for them at the front door when they walked up. Kyle's mum unlocked the door, and everyone hurried inside. They turned on the lights and saw a piece of paper had been taped to the door leading to the exam rooms.

"Looks like Angie fed the kittens at three a.m.," Dr Blake said, reading the note. She looked at Kyle and Mia. "Do you two need any help feeding them?"

"No thanks," Kyle said. "I think we're all set. Angie showed us what we need to do last night."

Dr Blake stopped in her office while Kyle and Mia went straight to the kittens' cage. The kittens were already awake and waiting for them.

Mia carefully moved the kittens from their cage back to the box and carried it into an exam room. While she mixed up the formula, Kyle cleaned out the cage and put fresh water in the dishes for the kittens so they wouldn't be thirsty.

When Kyle got to the exam room, his mum let Rex into the clinic. The dog went straight to the kitten box on the floor.

"I could hear him barking," his mum explained.

"Rex really likes the kittens," Kyle explained.

Kyle and Mia sat down on the floor with three bottles filled with formula. Rex stretched out in front of the open door to guard the kittens.

"You feed the boys," Mia said. "I'll feed Smokey."

"Smokey?" Kyle asked, looking over at her. "Is that the girl?"

Mia nodded and picked up the smallest kitten. "Yep," she said. "Since her fur is the colour of smoke."

Kyle picked up the larger of the two boy kittens. "What should we call her brothers?" he asked.

"Hmm. They're both orange," Mia said. "How about Tiger for the bigger one and Cheeto for the smaller one?"

"I like those names," Kyle said. "Time to eat, Tiger."

Tiger guzzled the formula. When it was gone, Kyle put the kitten back in the box and picked up Cheeto to feed him. When the second kitten finished his bottle, Smokey was still eating. She was smaller and weaker than her brothers, so she ate more slowly.

"She's almost done," Mia said.

"Okay," Kyle said. He checked the clock on the wall. He and Mia still had to eat breakfast before their school bus came. But when he turned to put Cheeto back in the box, Kyle gasped. "Tiger is gone!"

Cat worries

"How could you lose a kitten?" Mia asked
frantically. She dug through the towels in
the box to make sure Tiger wasn't hidden
somewhere inside. But he was nowhere to be
found.

"I didn't lose him!" Kyle insisted. "I put him
back in the box. He was just there a second
ago."

Kyle and Mia hunted under the chairs and behind the exam table.

"It's like he just disappeared!" Mia said, standing up and looking around the room in disbelief.

"Well he can't have got very far," Kyle said. "He's just a kitten. He has to be in here somewhere."

Suddenly they heard a quiet purring noise. Kyle and Mia looked at each other. It sounded like it was coming from the doorway across the room.

Kyle and Mia hurried over to where Rex lay, still protectively guarding the entrance to the exam room.

Kyle breathed a sigh of relief when he saw the source of the noise. Tiger was curled up against the dog's side, sound asleep and purring happily.

"Looks like the kittens like Rex as much as he likes them," Kyle said.

"I thought dogs and cats didn't get along," Mia said with a laugh.

After school, Kyle and Rex met Mia at her house. She came out the front door carrying a bottle of water and a bag of cat food in her arms. They had decided to go back over to the shed and see if the mother cat had returned yet.

"I really hope the mum is okay," Mia said to Kyle as they walked towards the shed. "I'm worried about the kittens, too. They need homes."

"Maybe someone at school will want one. We should take pictures of the kittens with us tomorrow," Kyle said as they hurried across the empty building site.

"Good idea," Mia said. "We should tell the whole class."

"That's a great plan!" Kyle said, grinning at his friend. "Do you think Mrs Lockwood will let us do that?"

Mia shrugged. "We won't know until we ask," she said.

They stopped in front of the shed. Mia crossed her fingers. Kyle peered inside. He didn't see any snakes or rats, so he reached in and pulled out the food dish.

"It's empty!" Mia said with a smile. "That means the mum cat has been here." She put more food in the dish and added, "I bet the cat will come back again, just like your mum said."

Kyle poured fresh water into the other dish. "I just hope it was the cat and not something else," he said.

"Uh-oh," Mia said with a gasp. She looked really worried. "I didn't even think about that."

The big pitch

The next day, Mia and Kyle brought some cute photos of the kittens to school. Before class started, they convinced Mrs Lockwood to let them talk to the other pupils.

"Kyle and Mia have an announcement to make," Mrs Lockwood said. "So, everyone, please pay attention."

Kyle took his place by the blackboard while Mia handed out pictures for the rest of the children to pass around. "Mia and I found three abandoned kittens on Monday afternoon," he said.

"Why were they abandoned?" someone asked.

"We think their mother left to go look for food," Kyle said. "Or something happened to her."

"The kittens were really small and weak, so we had to take them to Kyle's mum's vet clinic," Mia added.

"And now we have to find homes for them," Kyle said.

"I love this one!" Lucy said. She giggled and held up a picture of Rex cleaning one of the kittens with his tongue. The kitten's face was all scrunched up.

"And this one," Connor said, holding up a picture of Tiger sleeping next to Rex. "It looks like he's using your dog's ear as a blanket."

"That's Tiger," Kyle said. "We took that picture after he sneaked out of his box. I thought he was making a run for it!"

"When will they be old enough to take home?" Billy asked.

"You can have one at the end of the week," Kyle said. "They're about seven weeks old. My mum said they could go to their new homes at eight weeks."

"If you're interested, you can see them at Kyle's mum's clinic," Mia said. "The kittens have to get good homes, and we won't worry if you guys take them."

"They're cute, but I don't want a fur ball," Billy said. "I like creepy critters."

Ryan shook his head. "I can't take one," he said. "My sister already has a cat, and my parents don't want any more pets."

"My brother's snake gets loose sometimes," Lucy said. "I don't think it's a good idea to have a kitten in the house with a snake on the loose."

"I'd love a kitten, but my mum is allergic to cat hair," Emma said. "Sorry."

Kyle and Mia exchanged a worried glance. It seemed like everyone they talked to thought the kittens were adorable. But as cute as everyone thought they were, no one had offered to take one home.

As soon as they got home, Kyle and Mia hurried to the shed. The food dish was empty again, but there was still no sign of the mother cat.

They filled the dishes with more food and fresh water and rushed back to the clinic, just in case anyone from school showed up to see the kittens.

Nobody did.

"What are we going to do?" Mia asked when they sat down to feed the kittens. "The kittens can't stay here forever. They need homes."

"We'll think of something," Kyle said. "We have to."

8

The big kitty home hunt

When Kyle woke up on Thursday morning, he had a plan. He called Mia straight away. "Let's go to Mr J's Pet Haven," he said. "Maybe he can take the kittens. Or he'll know someone who wants one."

"Great idea," Mia said. "Let's go after school."

When Kyle and Mia walked into the shop that afternoon, Jethro, Mr J's pet parrot, was there to welcome them.

"Who's there?" Jethro squawked as they opened the door. "Go away!"

"That's bad for business, Jethro," Mr J said with a laugh. "It's a good thing everybody loves a cranky parrot."

"They love cute, little kittens more," Mia said.

"I'm hungry!" Jethro squawked.

Kyle gave the parrot a piece of cracker from the dish Mr J always kept on the counter. Then he said, "We have three kittens that need homes."

"We found them in an empty building," Mia explained. She pulled out three of the cutest pictures they'd taken and handed them to Mr J to look at. "Kyle's mum said they're almost seven weeks old."

"They are very cute," Mr J agreed, flipping through the photos.

"Could you sell them here?" Mia asked hopefully. "I bet lots of people would be interested!"

Mr J shook his head. "I'm sorry," he said. "I'd really love to help you out, but I only sell purebred kittens like Persians and Siamese here. You're welcome to put a picture and a sign on my bulletin board, though. Maybe someone will see it and want one."

Mr J gave them a piece of paper, and Kyle and Mia got to work making a sign. They chose a picture of all three kittens together and wrote the number for Dr Blake's clinic below.

When they were finished, they walked over to the bulletin board by the front door. Hopefully someone would see the flyer there. But there were already several flyers for free kittens.

"There are so many ads here!" Kyle said.

"I guess there are a lot of kittens that need homes," Mia said.

"We should post an ad anyway," Kyle said. "Maybe we should say that our kittens have been seen by a vet and had their shots. A lot of these other kittens probably haven't."

"It can't hurt," Mia said.

They added a line to their flyer and stuck it on the board along with all the other posted ads.

"Bye!" Jethro said as they walked out. "And don't come back!"

"Maybe we should put up a sign in your mum's clinic, too," Mia suggested as they left the pet shop.

Kyle shook his head. "She already has one posted," he said. "She and Angie and Lillian have been asking everyone who comes in if they're interested."

"Any takers?" Mia asked hopefully.

Kyle shook his head. "Not yet."

"What about putting up flyers around the neighbourhood?" Mia suggested. "That way people who don't have pets and don't have a reason to go to the pet shop or vet's office will see them."

"That's a great idea!" Kyle said. "We can make them on my computer. Let's go!"

A late addition

Kyle and Mia hurried back to his house and created a flyer about the kittens. They made sure the clinic's phone number was included. Then they printed out twenty copies.

"I hope this works," Mia said.

Rex tried to follow along behind them when Mia and Kyle headed downstairs.

"I think he's upset that we left him behind the past two days," Kyle said. "He wants to come, too."

Kyle grabbed Rex's leash, and they headed out the door. They were halfway down the block when Mia suddenly stopped. "Look!" she said, pointing across the street. "The mother!"

Kyle looked where Mia was pointing. Sure enough, there was a skinny cat sneaking out of the shed.

"I can't believe we forgot about her food!" Mia said.

"We're only a little late. And only because we were thinking about the kittens," Kyle said. "We can take her food first and then put up the signs."

"Works for me!" Mia said. "We'd better go back and get the stuff."

"Good idea," Kyle said. "Let's take Rex back to my house, too. We don't want him to scare her off."

They turned back down the street, and Mia ran to her house to get the cat food and water bottle for the mother. Kyle set the signs they'd made on a table on his front porch and put a rock on top of the pile so they wouldn't blow away.

Then he took Rex back inside and hung up his leash. Rex whined unhappily when he realized he was being left behind again.

"Sorry, boy," Kyle said. "No walk right now. We'll come and get you later."

Rex still wasn't happy about being left behind, but there was no choice.

A few minutes later, Mia came back out of her house carrying the cat supplies, and they hurried down the street. When they were a few feet from the shed, Kyle came to an abrupt halt.

"What?" Mia asked.

"I thought I saw something," Kyle whispered.

"You did!" Mia whispered back. She pointed at the skinny tabby disappearing behind the shed.

"I bet she was waiting for her dinner," Kyle said.

"Let's put food in the dish and wait," Mia said. "If we're quiet, she might come to us."

Kyle and Mia filled the dishes and set them outside the door. Then they sat and waited. A few minutes later, the cat came back. The children didn't move while she ate.

"Here, kitty, kitty, kitty," Mia said.

"Why does everyone call cats like that?" Kyle asked.

"Because cats think it means they'll get food," Mia said.

After the cat ate, she drank a little water and sat down to wash her face with her paw. When she finished, she walked right up to Mia and rubbed against her leg.

"She's not wearing a collar," Mia said. "I guess that means she doesn't have an owner. Looks like we have one more cat to find a home for."

10

Please, take a kitten!

Saturday morning was the last time Kyle
and Mia had to give the kittens formula. The
little cats were doing so well that they didn't
need it anymore. They could just eat their
kitten food and drink water.

"I really hope someone calls about the
kittens soon," Mia said. "I love taking care of
them, but Smokey, Tiger and Cheeto need real
homes."

"I know," Kyle agreed. "I thought those flyers would work straight away, but no one has come by to adopt them."

But that soon changed. At 9:30, Connor came to the vet's office with his mum.

"Are you here about the kittens?" Mia asked.

Connor nodded happily. "We came to get one," he said. "I talked to my mum about them, and she loves cats."

"I had a cat when I was growing up," Connor's mum told them. "She was a rescue cat, too. I really miss her. When Connor told me you had three rescue kittens looking for homes, I just couldn't resist."

Kyle and Mia led Connor and his mum to the back room of the clinic where the kittens were being kept.

"I want Tiger," Connor said as they walked up to the kitten's cage. "He's the one who climbed out of the box first, Mum."

"So he's smart and adorable!" Mrs Moss exclaimed as Mia handed the big, yellow kitten to Connor.

⌢⌢⌢

"One down and two to go," Kyle said when Connor and his mum had left with their new kitten.

"Three," Mia corrected him. "We have to find a home for the mother cat, too."

A few minutes later, the phone rang. "Dr Blake's Veterinary Clinic," Lillian answered. She paused, listening. "Yes, we still have two left, plus an adult cat."

"Was that someone calling about the kittens?" Kyle asked.

Lillian nodded. "It was a man looking for a kitten for his daughter," she said. "He saw one of your signs. They'll be by this morning."

Kyle and Mia high-fived each other. "I knew they'd work!" Mia said.

Thirty minutes later, the man and his daughter arrived. They played with the two remaining kittens for a few minutes before deciding to take Cheeto home. The little girl cuddled Cheeto close as they left.

After they left, Lillian moved the kitten box into the waiting room so Smokey wouldn't be lonely. The grey-and-white kitten climbed out of the box and used her kitten claws to climb up the receptionist's trouser leg. She immediately curled into a ball in Lillian's lap and went to sleep.

The clinic closed at noon for lunch, so Kyle and Mia decided to head next door to Kyle's house to check on Rex. When they came back after lunch, an elderly woman was sitting in the waiting room with Dr Blake. The mother cat was sitting in her lap, purring happily.

"Mrs Brown is going to take the mother," Dr Blake told them. "Her cat passed away last month."

"I need a new cat, and this one needs me," Mrs Brown said with a smile. "It's a perfect match."

"That's great news!" Mia exclaimed. She looked around the clinic, but she didn't see the last kitten anywhere. "Hey, where did Smokey go?"

"Lillian decided to take her home," Dr Blake said, smiling. "After Smokey took a nap on her lap earlier, she said she just couldn't resist."

"Excellent!" Kyle exclaimed. "All three kittens have homes!"

"And so does their mother!" Mia said happily. "Mission accomplished!"

"I'm so proud of you both for taking such good care of the kittens," Dr Blake said. "I know you'll miss them, but you did a great job finding good homes for all of them. You should be proud of yourselves."

The only one who didn't seem happy was Rex. He looked into the empty box and whined. Then he flopped down on the floor and rested his chin on his paws.

"I think Rex misses the kittens, too," Mia said.

"He'll get over it," Kyle said. "Watch." He opened the door and grabbed a spare leash off the wall. "Rex, do you want to go for a walk?" he asked.

Rex immediately jumped up and ran to Kyle. The dog was so excited, he panted and turned in circles.

Mia laughed. "Kittens?" she said. "What kittens?"

"Walks are more fun than kittens, huh, boy?" Kyle said as he snapped the leash on Rex's collar.

But Rex was already running out the door.

AUTHOR BIO

Diana G. Gallagher lives in Florida, USA, with three dogs, eight cats and a cranky parrot. She has written more than 90 books. When she's not writing, Gallagher likes gardening, garage sales and spending time with her grandchildren.

ILLUSTRATOR BIO

Adriana Isabel Juárez Puglisi has been a freelance illustrator and writer for more than twenty years and loves telling stories. She currently lives in Granada, Spain, with her husband, son, daughter, two dogs, a little bird and several fish.

GLOSSARY

abandoned (uh-BAN-duhnd) — deserted or no longer used

command (kuh-MAND) — to order someone to do something

examine (eg-ZAM-uhn) — to look carefully at something

investigate (in-VESS-tuh-gate) — to find out as much as possible about something

nervous (NUR-vuhss) — fearful or timid

protest (PROH-test) — to object to something strongly and publicly

DISCUSSION QUESTIONS

1. What would you have done if you found three abandoned kittens? Talk about some different solutions.

2. Why do you think Rex was so protective of the kittens? Talk about some possible reasons.

3. Where do you think the mother cat went when she left her kittens? Talk about some possibilities.

WRITING PROMPTS

1. Imagine that you're applying to get one of the kittens. Write a paragraph about why you would be a good owner.

2. If you were Kyle, how would you feel when all the kittens had found homes? Would you be happy or sad? Write a paragraph explaining your feelings.

3. What do you think the best part of having a kitten is? What is the hardest part? Write a paragraph about each.

CARING FOR YOUR CAT

Cats and kittens can make great pets, but like any animal, they need a responsible owner to help take care of them. See these tips for caring for your cat to make sure your pet stays safe and healthy!

- Make sure your cat wears a collar with an ID tag engraved with your address and phone number.

- Cats are carnivores, which means they eat meat. You can feed your cat wet food, dry food or a combination of the two.

- Feed your cat twice a day. Throw out any leftover wet food that hasn't been eaten after half an hour.

- Cats can sleep up to sixteen hours a day, so make sure that your cat has a cozy bed to curl up in.

- If your cat is an indoor cat, it will need a litter tray for going to the toilet. You should clean out your cat's litter tray daily.

Cats can't eat everything. Memorize this list of things to avoid for your cat:

- Chocolate

- Bones

- Milk

- Avocado

- Coffee

- Raisins and grapes

- Salt

- Garlic

- Onions, onion powder

Pet Friends Forever

READ THE WHOLE SERIES
and learn more about
Kyle and Mia's animal adventures!

Find them all at
www.raintree.co.uk

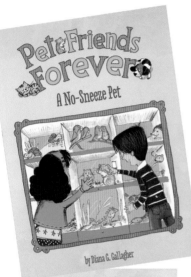

Pets Friends Forever
A No-Sneeze Pet

by Diana G. Gallagher

Pets Friends Forever
The Great Kitten Challenge

by Diana G. Gallagher

Pets Friends Forever
Mice Capades

by Diana G. Gallagher

Pets Friends Forever
The Doggone Dog